Trafalgar True

Written by Stephen Cosgrove
Illustrated by Robin James

A Serendipity™ *Book*

PSS!
PRICE STERN SLOAN

The Serendipity™ series was created by Stephen Cosgrove and Robin James

Copyright © 2002, 1980 Price Stern Sloan. All rights reserved.
Published by Price Stern Sloan
a division of Penguin Putnam Books for Young Readers,
345 Hudson Street, New York , New York 10014.

ISBN: 0-8431-4890-X

Revised Edition: 2004 printing

Dedicated to a dear friend Merrilynn Clark.
Over the years she has shared with me
her laughter and her joy for life.
Truly she is the strongest of the strong.

—Stephen

Beyond the horizon, farther than far, in the middle of the Crystal Sea, is a beautiful island called Serendipity. High on the mountains of the island in a small valley neither here nor there was a curious little meadow called Kurium.

It was a curious place because it was filled only with love and tenderness.

It was a curious place, too, because here lived a tender and gentle creature, Traflagar True. It was true that Trafalgar was a dragon. It was true that he was winged. But it was truer still that he was the most peaceful of creatures.

He lived for peace and peace he was.

It was his search for peace and quiet and gentleness that had brought him to Kurium in the first place. Kurium was filled with all things gentle, and the most gentle of the gentle were little furry creatures called Kith and Kin.

There was little difference between Kith and Kin; both had long bushy tails and big, pretty eyes. The only true difference was that the Kith had black fur with a long white stripe down the middle and the Kin had white fur with a black stripe. They spent their days quietly playing games in the meadow of Kurium.

All the while Trafalgar True sat beneath a tree and peacefully watched.

The gentleness of Kith and Kin alike brought him much pleasure.

It was in reward of that pleasure that Trafalgar True brought a gift to Kurium, a wonderful, beautiful gift. For, you see, Trafalgar found a magnificent, shimmering Sun Stone that had fallen from the sky. It was very rare and it could be said that on the island of Serendipity there was but one Sun Stone.

Filled with good intentions, Trafalgar carefully flew the stone back to the meadow of Kurium and left it there as a gift for both the Kith and Kin.

But it was a well-intentioned gift that was to bring much strife to the island and the creatures that lived there.

It wasn't long before the gentle Kith and Kin found the gift. The beauty of the Sun Stone did not go without notice. First there was just a Kith, and soon the Kith was joined by a Kin and then the Kin was joined by another Kith and soon the meadow filled with all the Kith and Kin.

At first they looked at the Sun Stone in quiet awe, and then a Kith pushed a Kin to get a better look and one thing led to another.

"Quit pushing," snapped a Kith to a Kin, "You can look at my Sun Stone in a minute."

"Your Sun Stone?" grumbled the Kin, "Think again fuzz face, it's my Sun Stone."

Kurium soon filled with the grumbling and rumbling of Kith and Kin as they argued over who owned the Sun Stone.

You would, as you read this story, hope that things would get better in quiet and gentle Kurium, but that was not to be. Kith and Kin continued their argument about who owned the Sun Stone and who should be allowed to view it and when.

Soon the meadow was filled with angry shouts and accusations.

Soon, Kith and Kin began acting in a way they had never acted before—mean and very spiteful. Why Kith even tripped Kin as they hurried to the Sun Stone.

Things could not have gotten much worse from a gift that was to bring joy, not strife.

Trafalgar True was sad beyond sad.

He had simply wanted to give the little creatures of Kurium a gift of joy, but instead the Sun Stone had brought nothing but anger and grief.

"Surely it will get better," he thought, a small blue tear slipping from his eye. "Kith and Kin will learn to share the beauty of the Sun Stone."

But it didn't get better, it got worse.

The Kith came up with a simple plan that would solve the issue of who owned the Sun Stone, using vines they would drag it to their part of the meadow. Then the Kin would have to ask permission to view the stone.

It was a good idea—too good of an idea. It was good enough that the Kin had the very same idea.

Each had vines wrapped around the Sun Stone as each tried to move it to their side of the meadow. They each pulled and, of course, the Sun Stone didn't move an inch.

Late that afternoon as Kith and Kin plotted and planned how to move *their* Sun Stone, a little Kinlett named Kitty stood before the stone. With a tear trickling down her cheek Kitty Kin cried, "I hate you Sun Stone. I wish you would go back where you came from!"

In the distance, sheltered in the trees at the edge of the meadow, a sad Trafalgar True listened.

Trafalgar knew that something must be done, and be done quickly before there was a war between Kith and Kin. It was obvious that they would never learn to share.

The very next morning, while Kith and Kin were still asleep Trafalgar grabbed the Sun Stone in his mighty arms and lifted it into the sky. He would take the Sun Stone home. He would fly it to the sun and then all would be at peace in the meadow of Kurium.

It wasn't but a moment later that Kith and Kin alike woke from their sleep to find the Sun Stone gone!

"I knew it! While we slept a Kin stole the stone!"

"Yeah, right!" snapped the Kin, "We all know it was the Kith who've got it!"

"No," said Kitty Kin, "It's Trafalgar True!"

Sure enough, they all looked up into the sky to see Trafalgar winging away. "Where are you going with our stone?" They cried.

"I'm taking the stone back to the sun," he shouted as he flew higher into the sky. "What cannot be shared by one cannot be shared by all. The Sun Stone belongs to no one!"

"But," said Kitty Kin, "Trafalgar will die if he flies the stone back to the sun!"

Kith looked at Kin, and Kin looked at Kith. Kitty Kin was right; Trafalgar true would surely die if he flew the stone back to the sun.

"Someone must do something!" said Kitty Kin.

"But who?" they asked in unison. "You? Me? Kith? Kin?"

"No, no," said the little Kinlett, "we must do this as one." Quickly she told them her plan.

Together Kith and Kin held furry little paws forming a gigantic circle.

They began singing out with one voice, "Trafalgar True! Trafalgar True! As one and all we beg of you! Please come back, we truly care. Please come back and we'll always share!"

They sang this over and over and finally Trafalgar looked down from high in the sky and slowly turned and flew back to the beautiful meadow of Kurium.

True to their words from that day forward Kith and Kin shared and shared alike. They shared the Sun Stone, their friendship, and their play.

From a distance Trafalgar watched in wonder. For all in all, he had given a much greater gift than he could ever imagine.

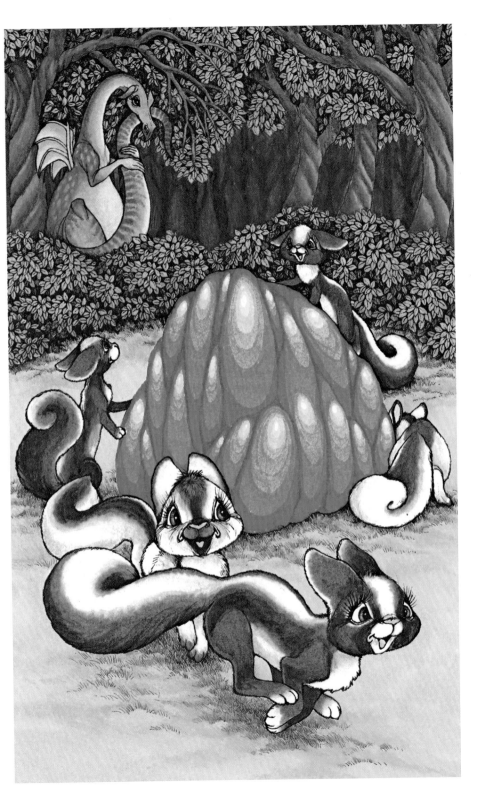

IF YOU'RE GOOD

AND IF YOU CARE,

LIKE KITH AND KIN

YOU CAN LEARN TO SHARE

Serendipity™ Books

Created by
Stephen Cosgrove and Robin James

Enjoy all the delightful books in the Serendipity™ Series:

Available wherever books are sold.

PSS!
PRICE STERN SLOAN